Aꝉ

By Rodger Beals

Illustrations by Cameron Beals

ISBN: 9781791691998

DEDICATION

Rodger Beals wrote this book in his last year of life. His goal was to entertain his grandchildren and anyone else looking for a wild west coast adventure. Max, Sunny, Sierra, Silver and Alexander, this book is for you.

Rodger Beals

CONTENTS

CHAPTER ONE:
SLUG RACE

Are people the same as other creatures? Perhaps even wondering this thought is something that only people do. Speech can't be the difference: whales speak, so do dolphins and don't ask a dog person about their pooch. The making of tools at first seems peculiar to people but monkeys make tools and so do crows; always up to something. Racing is the activity that really sets people apart from other creatures. People love to race. They race on foot, in vehicles, skiing down mountains, even shooting rifles while skiing down mountains. Eating hotdogs is a favorite, some prefer pie, putting things together, taking things apart. People are just nuts about racing and all other creatures have absolutely no interest unless, of course people decide to include them in races. People very much like doing this. Sometimes they sit on the creatures, horses are the most popular but elephants will do or even ostriches or sheep. Animals too small to carry a rider don't escape this particular passion of people, dogs are raced, rabbits, sometimes pigs. On Bowen Island, a small island in the Pacific Ocean at the mouth of Howe Sound, people didn't race animals. Bowenites, the people who lived on Bowen Island didn't hunt animals either and a lot of them wouldn't as a matter of choice, eat animals. Howe Sound is more beautiful than Puget Sound, a neighboring sound bigger and much better known. The two sounds shared more than just a neighborhood. They were both in the famous Ring of Fire that explained the huge volcanoes at the end of each waterway. It did not explain the big cities that people had built right next to the two volcanoes: Vancouver and Seattle. Vancouver's volcano was named Mount Garibaldi after some dead Italian politician. The Natives called it Nch'Kay meaning Grimy One. Seattle's volcano was called Mount Rainier after a British admiral. The Natives called it Tacoma.

Bowenites loved their fellow creatures and this explained why they did not race them. There were as many deer as people on Bowen Island, maybe more. There were no bears, mountain lions, coyotes or raccoons (although they all lived just across the water). The absence of these animals, predators all, was just fine with Bowenites who didn't like animals eating other animals. There were exceptions of course, there always are. Bald eagles lived on the tallest trees around the island and their diet consisted entirely of other animals. It was assumed they ate fish from the ocean and left the island's rabbits, mice and squirrels alone. This was fine with Bowenites. This assumption would not survive an examination of the bones surrounding an eagle's tree. Bowenfest was another exception to the island's rules. Bowenfest was a once a year, end of summer festival held on the fairgrounds of Bowen's only town, Snug Cove. The ferry from the mainland docked every hour in the town's narrow harbor. Snug Cove wasn't much of a town, it had a library, some restaurants, a general store and an elementary school but it was mostly deserted unless the ferry was arriving or a special event held. Bowenfest was the island's most special event and everyone on the island showed up. Many came to eat, listen to music, visit the exhibits and play games. Others came to prepare food, play music, display exhibits and officiate games. Principal Standish was an exhibitor at Bowenfest. If there was a prize for least visited exhibit he would win it every year. The principal was perplexed about this. Recycling was important, perhaps not exciting but certainly interesting; his green bin was for organics, the blue for plastic and metal, the brown for soiled diapers and he had items for the children to sort through and deposit and ribbons if they did so correctly. All he lacked was visitors. Most of the children, many of them Principal Standish's own students were crowded around the very next exhibit. Its one sign was a dirty chalkboard with a hastily scribbled "SLUG RACE" on it. This was Bowen Island's only race, the one exception to the island's no racing animals rule. Bowen Island had more slugs than deer; they were large, some as big as hotdogs and black or brown and occasionally green although green slugs were not raced; it was thought they were endangered even though neighboring islands had them by the bucket-load. The rules of the slug race were simple: one slug per person and it had to have a name that was written on another chalkboard. The racetrack was a long piece of broad plywood divided into sixteen lanes. Each lane had wooden sides about as high as a slug was long. It was hoped the sides would keep each slug in his own lane but often slugs had their own ideas. Slug owners were allowed to place a piece of 'slug food' at the end of racetrack just beyond the red colored finish line. Each contestant had his or her own theory about slug food and pepperoni, stale donut, celery and peanut butter waited for the few slugs that crossed the finish line. Principal Standish shook his head and pursed his lips. Nothing was learned from such foolishness and it appeared that some adults were betting on the outcome of the race--definitely not suitable for children. The noise of the crowd grew louder as the slugs were positioned and the racing adjudicator placed the whistle to her lips. The shrillest voices belonged to twin girls. He knew them well; students at his school, almost in trouble frequently which was different than frequently in trouble; one day he would surely see them in his office.

"Slither like the wind, you black beauty," yelled Eloise, her hair cut shorter but otherwise identical to her sister, Charlie.

"No one can catch you, Dread Pirate Roberts," yelled Charlie who had named the slug. The race started and it was instant pandemonium. The noise of the racers explained why no one heard the murder of crows screeching overhead. The slugs who had spent the last few hours, some even days in jars and plastic tubs sprinted across the starting line, their newfound freedom giving them almost caterpillar-like speed. This didn't last. Only two of the sixteen stayed in its lane, the other fourteen almost immediately climbed up the wooden sides, reversed course or refused to move at all. Their owners leaned over the racetrack and yelled or pointed toward the finish line, careful not to touch a racer or the track that meant instant disqualification (the adjudicator was a librarian). Without warning (except for the crows) the ground began to shake violently and suddenly opened up down the middle of the fairground. A huge crack headed straight toward the slug race and the crowd that had stopped yelling at their slugs and was now screaming in terror. The crack stopped just in front of the race and then streaked off to the left.

"Every man for himself," yelled Principal Standish just before he and his exhibit were swallowed by the crack. He was never seen again.

CHAPTER TWO: YAP

Yap is an island on the other side of the world twice as large as Bowen. Like Bowen it is on the Ring of Fire, that giant line of volcanoes that circles the Pacific Ocean. The two little islands are made of volcanic rock, Yap because it actually is a volcano and Bowen because it is so close to one. The volcanic rock explains why farming and vegetable gardening are frustrating activities for the Yapese and the Bowenites. But people must eat and make a living. The Yapese people are famous for inventing the biggest coins the world has ever seen to encourage fishing and trading of those fish. The coins were made from an exotic non-volcanic rock they found on a nearby island. The largest coins were as big as the huts that the ancient Yapese lived in. One Yapese sunk his boat while carrying his treasure home. The Bowenites use a coin called the Loonie. It fits nicely in a pocket but some people still find it too large. A Loonie can buy you just about anything at the Knick Knack Nook. The Nook, a used everything store is where most Bowenites buy clothes, toys, jewelry, bikes, kitchen stuff and anything else they need. If the Nook doesn't have what you want, just wait and it will be there soon enough. Some Bowenites buy things at the Nook and then sell those things for much more money to people who don't live on the island. Bowen Islanders make more money doing this than the Yapese ever did selling fish. All the children that live on Bowen shop at the Nook. They start young, some before they can walk and they all begin with toys. The toys are not new, of course, but they are cheap and a small basket can be filled for less than a Loonie. Older children buy their clothes at the Nook or at least their parents buy the clothes for them. Most of the students at the Bowen Island Community School (BICS) were wearing something from the Nook on the first day of school. This year there was no talk of summer adventures, new kids or speculation about what teacher was pregnant. Everyone was talking about the earthquake that had swallowed their principal, where they were and what they had been doing when it happened.

"Silence!" A voice boomed across the auditorium/ gymnasium. The speaker was a huge and ugly man. His head barely fit under doorways and long greasy black hair fell below his rounded shoulders. A dark beard covered half his face and belly spilled over his belt. The seated students fell silent. "I am Mr. Grimes your new principal." Principal Grimes smiled grimly at his students and gave them a few seconds to look at him before continuing. "Students will no longer talk during assembly. I have zero tolerance."

Eloise bent down to tie her shoe and whispered sarcastically, "He seems friendly."
When she sat up Principal Grimes looked right at her and smiled evilly even though he couldn't possibly have heard. "We will all bow our heads for ten seconds to honor Principal Standish's tragic death. You may raise your heads," he said after five seconds.

"That was not ten seconds," said Charlie while her head was still bowed.

"I have one order of business and then you are dismissed and may go to class. Starting today I will teach the Grade Seven class Environmental Studies every morning. You may go."

"Oh no," Eloise signed to her sister. Their Sixth Grade class had taken American Sign Language for an entire month the previous year.

"I bet he smells," Charlie signed back.

Principal Grimes pointed his huge right hand at the sisters. "Come to my office after school," he signed and laughed. Two of his front teeth were gold.

Principal Grimes sat down at his desk in the Grade Seven Environmental Studies classroom. As he reached into his briefcase the smell of rotten eggs and sulfur reached the first row of desks. "You may open a window," he said to the students struggling unsuccessfully to keep their noses from wrinkling. "I have a medical condition," he added and shrugged. Bowenite children were a friendly and accepting bunch and most smiled faintly in sympathy at their new principal and his medical condition. Not Eloise and Charlie. They did not believe him and found his shrug insincere.

"You may take notes while I speak; you may not talk or sign," he said looking at the sisters.

Eloise bent down to tie her shoe again. "He's creepy."

"I suggest you use a double knot, Eloise," said Principal Grimes holding the class list in his hand but not looking at it. "That way you won't have to keep tying your shoe."

Charlie coughed into her hand and said quietly, "Very creepy."

Principal Grimes stood up and walked slowly down the center aisle of desks. His smell followed. "The law of the jungle is the law of the world. Survival of the Fittest is scientific fact. Animals, including humans, eat other animals, insects, or plants. This is how life exists and thrives on our beautiful planet."

Eloise raised her hand.

"Yes, Eloise. I assume you have something to say that is about the Survival of the Fittest."

"Animals don't eat other animals on Bowen Island."

"I can assure you they do," said Principal Grimes laughing unkindly.

"There are no predators on our island."

"Of course there are. Man is a predator, cats are predators, as are dogs; you are mistaken and what you say are the words of a child. Soon you will be an adult and if you study and listen to your teachers you will go to university. It is time to put away your childish thoughts and see the world as it really is."

"I've lived here all my life," said Charlie without putting up her hand, "and I've never seen an animal eat another animal on Bowen Island."

Principal Grimes laughed again. "Sit down girls."

That night a mountain lion swam across Howe Sound and ate Mrs. Fletcher's poodle.

CHAPTER THREE:
COMOVA

Yap Island had one more thing in common with Bowen Island besides the Ring of Fire and large coins. Both islands were visited from time to time by killer whales or orcas as scientists and learned people liked to call them. Humans have long studied killer whales and every year they learn a little more. If they keep at it they might discover that orcas have been studying them as well. Killer whales have been doing this since the first boat was launched by the first human thousands of years ago. Were humans dangerous those ancient orcas wondered and how did they taste. Human tastiness was only of interest to two of the three types of killer whales: the Transients and the Offshores as the scientists would later call them. Transients never stayed in one place for long and only ate mammals. Humans are mammals. The Offshores live far out in the ocean away from land and do not like to be studied. Not much is known about them. The third type of orcas was called the Residents because they stayed in one place. Residents eat fish and nothing else. Humans, the Transients and the Offshores discovered, did not taste good and they were removed from the list of tasty mammals. This list included seals, sea lions, dolphins and sharks although sharks are not mammals. Sharks also like to eat seals, sea lions and dolphins. Killer whales don't like to share so they added sharks to their list and eat them at every opportunity even the huge Great White Shark. Transients are slightly bigger than the Residents but not as smart and don't talk as much. Transients and Residents don't like each other. If both groups liked the same food there would certainly be trouble. Orcas live in large groups called pods. Grandmothers are always in charge of the pod. Perhaps humans should try this.

Apodaca was in charge of the largest Resident killer whale pod in the northern Pacific Ocean. She had twelve daughters and ten sons. Her daughters lived in the pod and they too had daughters who lived in the pod. Apodaca's sons and grandsons were scattered around the ocean, some attached to different pods, others trying to get attached to other pods. They might as well be Transients thought Apodaca disapprovingly of her sons and grandsons. She missed them but at least Bruno, her youngest son stayed with the pod. Perhaps there was something wrong with him. He always was an odd one. Apodaca was faced with the never before faced problem of leaving one of her offspring in charge of the pod while she took care of some private business. Bruno, of course was out of the question. He was male which automatically disqualified him, which was good given his temperament. The proper choice would be one of his sisters; Apodaca's eldest, Winnifred came to mind but she was a ninny and aging hadn't made her less so. It would have to be Lucy, level headed and respected by all. Apodaca still had to speak to the pod. She dreaded this normally pleasant task; she was tired and anticipated an unhappy pod hearing her news. Comova had come to her in the in what was ordinarily the middle of her sleep. Apodaca had been awake since. His voice was deep as it always was, vibrating her entire head. It was not a discussion; Apodaca said nothing other than 'Yes, Lord' a handful of times. Comova was not her master but she owed him fealty and obedience ever since she became leader of the pod. Apodaca was the queen of the ocean but Comova was a volcano and could spit fire and rip holes in the earth.

Apodaca slipped into the calm still warm waters of Snug Cove, Bowen Island's only town. Howe Sound was a part of her pod's territory and Bowen Island was Apodaca's favorite of the Sound's many islands. She liked the fish, she liked the beaches and she liked the people. The fish were delicious, the beaches filled with small rocks suitable for scratching barnacles off a belly but it was difficult to put a fin on why she liked the people.

Bowen Island is of course part of Canada and Canadians are the very best of all at lining up. They are also nice. If one bumps into a Canadian in a crowded market the Canadian will always apologize; Canadians are that polite. Unless when playing hockey or confronted with illegal behavior in a line. Canadian lines can be as simple as taking turns or so complex that people from other countries are baffled. The ferry line up on Bowen even baffles Canadian visitors to the island. Cars are to line up in a single line except when there are two lines. There are frequently two lines. You may park your car in the ferry line up but don't block the parked cars that are beside the ferry line up. You may park your car on the unmarked road but don't park on the faded crossed lines on the road. If you can't see the faded crossed lines ask a local Bowenite what to do. These are the easy rules. Apodaca had no plans to ever use the ferry and a car for her was out of the question.

A harbor seal was dozing against the dock and Apodaca submerged and swam underneath it. Apodaca surfaced as close to the still slumbering seal as possible, bared her teeth and let a noisy blast of air and seawater out of her blowhole. The seal opened its big brown eyes and screamed, "Don't eat me!"

Apodaca laughed, "I thought animals didn't eat animals on Bowen Island."

"The ocean is not the island," stammered the seal trying to regain his composure.

"Then, I can eat you," said Apodaca clicking her teeth.

"You're a Resident, you only eat fish."

"You smell like fish."

"So do you. Why are you here? The ferry is coming soon. You should leave."

"I'm looking for two girls, twins. Seals are always poking around so I thought I'd ask you."

"Seals are curious and known for their sense of humor which is why I can tell you that your prank was not funny."

"I'm still laughing."

"Cruelty is not humor."

"I apologize. Now, where would I find the twins."

"They kayak every day to school while it's warm and the wind isn't blowing. They launch their boat at Scarborough Beach. Try not to scare them."

CHAPTER FOUR: LITTLE ORCA ANNIE

Little Orca Annie was Apodaca's favorite granddaughter.

This was surprising because Little Orca Annie's mother, God rest her soul, was Apodaca's least favorite daughter. She was disobedient, headstrong and foolish which probably explained her early death at Skookumchuck Narrows. Little Orca Annie, a mother herself now was also disobedient, headstrong and foolish but in a nice way. Every year Apodaca took her pod to Skookumchuck Narrows for fun and giggles. The mighty Pacific Ocean tide ripped though the small opening in the rock, the Narrows, and white fast moving water was everywhere. Killer whales loved it and as long as they stayed away from the dangerous rocks everything was good. The dangerous rocks were close together and a careless whale could get stuck between them underwater and drown. Little Orca Annie's mother suffered such a fate. Both of the dangerous boulders were volcanic rock and had been launched from nearby Mount Garibaldi many years ago. Apodaca had taken her orphan granddaughter under her fin after the accident and tried to be a mother to her but Annie's grief was too much and she wandered off as sad orcas sometimes do. This was when she met humans who rescued her, nursed her back to health and taught her their language. They also taught her jokes. These she learned from two people who cleaned the ocean enclosure where she lived in Manchester, Washington State. Her favorite jokes were puns, limericks and knock-knock jokes. One of the humans taught her this:

There once was a sick killer whale
Who sat all day on her tail
She only ate fish
When served on a dish
By a man with a bucket and pail

Limericks were the best Little Orca Annie thought and when the humans took her in a fast boat all healthy and fat back to her pod in Howe Sound she taught her grandmother and all the other killer whales the jokes she had learned as well as the human language. Apodaca was overjoyed to have her back and very much appreciated the jokes. Orcas love a good joke. The American and Canadian English that she learned had never been useful.

Scarborough Beach was about a twenty minute paddle from Snug Cove although Charlie and Eloise always parked their kayak in Deep Bay which was closer, a short walk from school and not as busy as Deep Cove which had the ferry of course, water taxis and the occasional seaplane. Deep Bay was practically deserted in September; the tourists in their boats who liked to moor in the free and sheltered water all gone. The girls were paddling slowly taking their time and talking.

"I still can't believe Killer got eaten," said Charlie. Killer was Mrs. Fletcher's poodle and the news had travelled fast around the island. Many sightings of the mountain lion responsible had been phoned into the Bowen Island Royal Canadian Mounted Police detachment even though the big cat had swum back to the mainland immediately after its supper.

"It was like Principal Grimes knew," said Eloise whispered. Sound carried on the open water and one always had to be careful talking on a small island where everyone knew everyone's business.

"Oh, he knew," said Charlie who was preparing to launch into a theory about shape shifting when a huge rogue wave suddenly swamped their kayak and dumped them both in the warm water of the bay. The girls were wearing their life jackets and their backpacks were safe and dry in their boat's waterproof bulkheads.

Apodaca, who had created the wave with her tail surfaced between the girls and said, "Surprise!" She did like a joke. The girls had seen killer whales many times before and didn't believe they were in danger. On the other hand Mrs. Fletcher's poodle probably hadn't been worried about mountain lions. "I just want to talk," said Apodaca, "Perhaps you should climb back into your kayak first."

"You speak," said Eloise.

"Since I was a calf. My name is Apodaca."

"How is it possible that we understand each other," said Eloise climbing in after her sister.

"An acquaintance of mine has rather special powers," continued Apodaca. "I don't know if it's magic but close enough. We're all going to understand each other for a while."

"An acquaintance," asked Eloise? "Another killer whale?"

"Never really met him. I think he's a volcano."

"Okay," said Charlie who was feeling a little cranky because she was soaking wet and late for school, "why are you here and did you have to dump us into the ocean."

"There's a crisis afoot."

"Everything seems pretty normal," said Charley, "except for you talking."

"Didn't you just have an earthquake, lose a principal and last night Mrs. Fletcher's poodle got eaten."

"Yeah," said both girls.

"That's the crisis."

CHAPTER FIVE: SPELUNKING

Yap Island has been conquered many times by different countries. For a time both Germany and Spain wanted it badly for no particular reason. They almost went to war but instead let the Pope decide for them. The Pope was the religious leader for the Spanish and in a decision that surprised no one except the Germans, gave Yap to Spain; the Yapese were not consulted. A few years later the Spanish sold it to the Germans. The Pope may have gotten something from the sale but the Yapese got nothing. In the First World War the English took Yap Island from the Germans and then gave it to the Japanese; the Yapese were not consulted. In the Second World War the Americans took the island from the Japanese. The Yapese found out that there are advantages to being invaded by Americans. So did the Japanese; the Americans made sure the island had electricity, water and sanitation. A hospital, schools and grocery stores came next. By the time Americans left it was nice enough for even an American to live there and that's what usually happens. American soldiers would fall in love with local women, get married and settle down. Jason Goser's grandfather was one of those soldiers and his grandmother was a local woman. Jason's grandfather started a hotel and marina that never did very well because in those days it was hard to get to Yap Island. Peter Goser, Jason's dad did much better and turned the marina into a scuba diving resort where people could stay and be taken by boat to the best diving areas Yap Island had to offer. Jason had driven the boat, since he was twelve. He was nineteen now and an expert scuba diver. He often took groups of divers down under the water to look at sunken ships from World War Two and the many beautiful fish that swum in the warm Pacific Ocean waters. Jason found scuba diving boring. He thought of himself more as a spelunker, a word the ancient Greeks made up to describe somebody crazy enough to explore caves. Spelunking is very dangerous except for Jason and some other crazy spelunkers not dangerous enough. Underwater spelunking was just about right for Jason and he had found the perfect cave to explore near Yap Island's volcano. Steam and bubbles occasionally came out of the narrow hole in the rocks about twenty feet below the ocean surface. Everyone on the island knew about it and everyone stayed away; it was obviously a path to a quick death. Jason's first dive into the underwater cave had not gotten very far. He ran out of light and couldn't see anything. Today he brought a very bright underwater light that would last for hours. No one knew what he was doing. Armed with his new light Jason squeezed through the entrance of the cave. Immediately, it narrowed and turned down. Jason pulled himself along with his gloved hands rather then using his big flippers. The cave shaft turned up and then narrowed even more. Jason knew he would not fit. This was not uncommon when spelunking. Normally, a spelunker would use a hammer and chisel to chip away the rock and make the opening bigger. Underwater spelunking required a different solution. Jason slipped his scuba tank off his back and held it in front. Now, he could fit. As he scraped his way through the small opening Jason wondered briefly where he could turn around to get out of the cave. The shaft continued to head upward and as it did it got larger and larger; plenty of room to turn around. Jason slung his tank back on his back and kicked with his fins. He was excited. Abruptly, the underwater cave ended and Jason popped his head out of the water into the air of a large cavern. He pulled himself onto a ledge and cautiously removed his mask. The air smelled faintly but was breathable. He took off his tank and fins and moved the light of his torch along the walls of the cavern. There was nothing to see but in the middle of the cavern was a small pool of clear water. Jason walked over the jagged rock of the cavern floor to the pool and sniffed the still water. It smelled fresh with no hint of the ocean. Jason dipped his cupped hand in and tasted it. Instantly, he fell to the rocks unconscious. When he woke an hour later as a crab nibbled his big tore. he did not notice the bumps and bruises on his forehead. He calmly put on his scuba diving equipment, climbed back into the cave and swam back to his little boat that was anchored above. Jason took his little boat back to his family's resort, wrote a note for his parents and took his father's sailboat. The note said: Going to Canada. Don't worry about me. Love Jason. P.S. Dad, I've borrowed your boat.

CHAPTER SIX: GOBSMACKED

Ferdinand Magellan, a Portuguese man, is famous for many things. He proved the world wasn't flat when he became the first person to sail around it. All the wise people at the time, especially the Pope, also the religious leader of the Portuguese, told him he would fall off the edge of the earth and suffer a terrible death. Magellan also discovered the Strait of Magellan, a quick way to get through South America without having to go around. In the Strait of Magellan he discovered the Willawaw. The Willawaw did almost kill him. It heeled over his ship, the Trinidad and nearly pooped it. The Strait of Magellan is also on the Rim of Fire and as Ferdinand carefully sailed his ship through the uncharted water he passed several volcanoes. In such cold ocean waters, when conditions are just right all the air will fall off the top of tall volcanoes and rush down to the water below. At the other end of the world, in Howe Sound another tall volcano existed and the conditions were also right for a Willawaw or Squamish as the local people called it. Squamish meant 'mother of winds' in a language still spoken around the area and was also the name of a town at the narrow tip of Howe Sound. The strong wind came in gusts of two or three and when they were as strong as a hurricane could be dangerous to sailors or kayakers but at the moment they were not bothering Professor Diefenbaker Stone at all. "Volcanic, volcanic, sedimentary," he said as he tossed rocks into Scarborough Bay.

"Watch where you're throwing those," said Apodaca who was far enough out in the water to be in no danger but wanted to strike up a conversation.

"Even when I was young and playing baseball every weekend I could not throw far enough to hit you."

"You're not gobsmacked to be talking to a whale," said Apodaca very pleased to use this word properly and for the first time.

"I've been losing my mind for the last five years so the doctors tell me," answered the professor as he picked up three more rocks and muttered 'sedimentary, volcanic and a piece of brick, I believe' before throwing them into the ocean.   "Dogs talk, cats seem to be very witty, I talk to myself; a talking whale does not strike me as odd."

"Then a meeting where most of the animals on Bowen Island show up and talk won't bother you."

"I must be Alice in Wonderland, no not Alice, probably the Mad Hatter."

"Two girls will also be in attendance, twins actually."

"All the better; they're my granddaughters don't you know, not by blood, their father is my wife's son, if you can follow that complicated lineage."

"I'm the matriarch of an orca pod."

"You must meet my wife."

"Grandpa," said Charlie as she came down steep wooden stairs to Scarborough Beach. "What are you doing here."

"Classifying rocks and talking to a killer whale."

"Oh, then you've met Apodaca," said Eloise who was right behind her sister.

"No introductions have been made," said the professor with slight disappointment, "Although it was not I who initiated the conversation."

"How silly," Charlie said. "Grandpa, I mean Professor Diefenbaker Stone this is Apodaca."

"He told me he was the Mad Hatter," said Apodaca.

"We can't have our meeting in this crazy wind," said Eloise.

"It will stop within the hour," said the professor.

"How can someone know this," said Apodaca. "Are you a volcano?"

"I am a scientist or, at least I used to be. Also, I used to be a windsurfer. They called me the Wind Kuhuna because I always knew when the Squamish winds would blow."

"Grandpa, you're all wet," said both girls tugging at his arms. "Come up to the house and get changed.

"Don't be long," said Apodaca. "The meeting starts as soon as the setting sun is on the mountains."

CHAPTER SEVEN: EVIL AFOOT

Ireland is another island in another ocean. It doesn't have volcanoes or killer whales and isn't part of this story. It does have an interesting people who like to travel. Irish people are said to like potatoes, the color green, Leprechauns, Saint Patrick's Day and politics. Everywhere they go they name things after places they like from their home, the Emerald Island. On Bowen they named the only good lake on the island Killarney Lake after some place in Ireland. Bowen's Killarney Lake doesn't look at all like Ireland. It's flat, not rocky and is dammed up by a large family of beavers. Ireland has no beavers although the Irish liked wearing beaver hats for a while. Wearing beaver hats was a popular fashion two centuries ago. It was tough on the beavers in Canada where most beavers live and for a few short years supplying the world with beaver hats was how almost everyone in Canada made money. Like every fashion craze it stopped suddenly and so did Canada's beaver economy. Those were some tough years but Canada recovered and so did its beaver population. Today, the beaver is Canada's national animal and can be found on some coins although not the Loonie. The truth is beavers are somewhat of a pest, always chewing down trees and damming up every river and creek they find. 'Busy As A Beaver' is a saying and no truer saying can be found. Beavers are always busy when they're awake at night managing the waterways they've created, mostly swamps and shallow ponds and lakes.

Killarney Kit was awake well before the sun would go down and he didn't care for it. People were still walking the circle trail around the lake and most of them had dogs. Kit didn't like dogs or people. Kit wasn't dumb but he didn't do a lot of thinking. Things just popped into his head. Dam the creek, chew down this tree were things his head told him to do. This morning his head told him he had to go to Scarborough Beach. This thought he didn't like. Kit didn't like walking on land and he was absolutely sure he wouldn't like the ocean. His wife and sons and newly arrived kits were all still sleeping in the many rooms of his magnificent beaver lodge. Kit always took time to admire the lodge and when he did his mind would make him add a few more branches and a lot more mud to it. Today however, the lodge began to shake before he could properly admire it. The water of his pond rippled. Steam rose from the surrounding swamp. The steam stunk worse than skunk. Kit really didn't like skunks. People and their dogs screamed, barked, ran back to their cars and left. The shaking and steam stopped. Kit waddled onto the Killarney Lake Park path and headed toward the ocean.

"It's a fissure, not an earthquake but the island has opened up beneath the water," said Professor Stone in his dry clothes after Kit told his story about the shaking and steam of Killarney Lake. Kit stood on a large driftwood log scowling at the deer, squirrels, dogs, cats, eagles, crows and even skunks that had come for the meeting on Scarborough Beach. The mountains across the Sound were a brilliant golden pink as the setting sun shone on them. The meeting had just started.

"Evil is afoot," said Apodaca loudly from out in the water. "I'm afraid your peaceful island is about to become a battleground."

"We'll just leave," said the eagles to the cheers of the other birds.

"Evil will follow," said Apodaca.

"Who are the bad guys," said Charlie.

"The evildoers will be revealed to me tonight," said Apodaca. "I have another meeting."

"Can we come," Eloise asked.

"I will inquire."

CHAPTER EIGHT: PRETTYBOY

"Can my friends, Charlie and Eloise attend our meeting, Comova."

"Ah, the Sisters; It's been a long time."

"I don't believe you've met," Apodaca said cautiously.

"Vanity, Apodaca, do you know what vanity is," Comova said.

"Never heard of it."

"Then I must tell you a story."

"Please, no just tell me what the word means."

"It is the shortest of stories, Apodaca. Compose yourself. I will start at the beginning."

"Perhaps just the end of the story and a definition of Vanity."

"The sun and the moon do not care for each other. Did you know? I thought not. They are not friends of mine, but I knew them both in early days. The moon is vain, all bright and close and for the longest time pretended to be this world's creator. 'I move the oceans', the moon would say which of course is true. The sun got sick of it, froze most of the oceans and said to the moon while pointing at the frozen water 'Move this' which brings me to my story."

"This isn't the story," Apodaca whined.

"The waters in Howe Sound became frozen and the ice grew and grew. Look about you, Apodaca as you swim. The mountains that tower above are rounded, worn smooth by that ice. Only the very highest peaks are jagged as a mountain should be and escaped the ice. The Lions, which I call the Sisters, Mount Harvey, and Brunswick Mountain around us today remained jagged and looked down and saw nothing but frozen wasteland."

"Do you mean the sun and the moon are alive?"

"Try to keep up, Apodaca. Everything is alive. You are, after all, talking to a volcano."

"Everything was frozen?"

"Almost everything was frozen. Prettyboy as I call him, or Mount Garibaldi as you call him was a very young volcano who wanted to erupt and build his cone to be the biggest--bigger even than my splendid cone. The older volcanoes of whom I count myself one, advised against it."

"Couldn't you just have told him no."

"Volcanoes don't give orders or have rules, we make suggestions."

"You're pretty bossy with me."

"We don't give orders to other volcanoes and certainly not the moon or sun; whales, humans and regular mountains are another matter."

"Why do you call him Prettyboy?"
"We call him Prettyboy, because he's actually quite ugly. It's volcano humor. Clever, is it not?"

"It sounds stupid and cruel."

"Perhaps, but it makes us laugh and it certainly bothers Prettyboy. You are interrupting far too much, Apodaca."

"I was hoping you were done."

"Prettyboy erupted in spite of our good advice and spewed lava and rocks everywhere. The lava even melted some of the ice but the sun would not allow this and made it even colder."

"I'm amazed the twins haven't said anything yet," said Apodaca.

"Oh, they can just hear us, they just can't speak. Your interruptions are quite enough."

"This must be killing them. Please let them talk."

"Very well."

"Is Prettyboy a bad guy," both girls yelled.

"Of course he is."

"Maybe because you tease him," said Eloise.

"Teasing is good for a volcano; good for everyone."

"So, what is Vanity," asked Charlie.

"Prettyboy's lava rocks and mud all ended up on the ice that surrounded his small cone. It did not run down and build his cone up the way he had hoped. Later, when the sun got tired of punishing the moon and warmed up, the ice, mud and dried lava fell and was washed away. Prettyboy was left hideous and very angry. Being beautiful is the most important thing in the world to him. That, girls and whale, is Vanity."

"I liked your story, Comova," said Apodaca, "but this vanity doesn't really sound evil."

"Ah, but vanity can create evil, it often does."

"Is it going to with Prettyboy," Eloise asked.

"It already has. Prettyboy has a plan to claim his beauty. Howe Sound is his domain. There is little I can do to help. Besides, he has friends."

CHAPTER NINE: SURVIVAL OF THE FITTEST

A nearly windowless gray van pulled in the parking lot of Crippen Park taking up two spots and spraying gravel onto the grass. Principal Grimes jumped out and slammed his door. He carried a clipboard and wore a black whistle around his neck. The BIM school bus carefully entered the turnaround behind him, came to a slow stop and opened its front door.

"By twos," Principal Grimes barked into the bus, "in alphabetical order and line up in front of the bridge." The bridge was a small concrete and metal walkway that separated the fresh water lagoon from the ocean waters of Deep Bay. Water from the lagoon spilled out through openings in the bridge that was really more of a dam. On the ocean side of the bridge was an elaborate salmon ladder of steps filled with gently flowing water. Huge salmon leapt from step to step until they reached the top where they could tumble exhausted into the still waters of the lagoon.

"You have to leave immediately," Principal Grimes said to a woman sitting on a stool on the bridge. An easel stood in front of her and she was holding a dripping paintbrush in the air and frowning at her canvas. She set her paintbrush down and slowly took a pipe from her shirt pocket and clamped it in her teeth.

"There is no smoking in any park on the island," said Grimes walking toward her.
The woman stood, took her pipe out of her mouth and pointed its stem at the Principal.

"There has been no tobacco in this pipe for over thirty years. It helps me think and I point it at things I don't like."

Charlie and Eloise who were standing behind their principal waved at the woman and both whisper-yelled, "Hi Grandma."

"We are about to have a lesson. If you won't leave I insist you be quiet."

"I'm painting," said the twins' grandmother, "I insist you stay out of my sight."

"Observe the salmon, students" said Grimes ignoring the woman. "They are returning to the stream where they were born years ago after traveling around the ocean. If you will look into the trees you will see seagulls waiting to feast on the salmon's dying bodies; raccoons, bear, coyotes and even members of the Native community are waiting in other streams across the Sound all ready to eat them. This, right before you eyes, is the survival of the fittest."

"You call this a lesson, you ninny," said the woman, standing and pointing her pipe again. "If the magic of the salmon is nothing but survival of the fittest to you, then you are a fool."

"I am the Principal of the school and a man of science. Magic is nonsense and does not exist."

"Magic is everywhere. Explain how these amazing fish know to return to their place of birth, all at the same time. And why do they do it. Please tell me, man of science."

"The science is not all known and complicated certainly beyond one who knows as little as you."

"I know who you are," said the woman loudly, taking a step toward Principal Grimes. "Be gone!" She yelled and closed her eyes.

Grimes staggered backwards. "Back into your bus," he commanded his students, turned on his heels and ran to his van. He jumped in and slammed the door. Five excited coyotes sprang from the back seat of the van. "Get back," Grimes snarled and the coyotes whimpered and slunk away.

CHAPTER TEN: KNICK KNACK NOOK

Fashion has cycles just like the earth has seasons. And there are rules. Daughters don't wear what there mothers wear or have worn, although the reverse isn't always true. Granddaughters might wear what their grandmothers have but the grandmother must be fairly old. Some fashion cycles are quite short. Scientists have studied them. There is a lot of money to be made in fashion. The first stage is the introduction, when a few famous people are wearing a particular item. Next comes the rise and peak of the fashion when everyone must have it and it flies off the shelves in stores. Decline follows when people tire of the item and those that first bought no longer wear if. A state of out of fashion is the final stage.

The fascinator is immune to these rules and cycles. First worn by Marie Antoinette, a one-time queen of France who lost her crown among other things. The fascinator is so wonderful that it cannot go out of fashion, daughters will wear those of mothers and stores will always have them in stock. A fascinator is a tiny hat worn on the front of the head. It covers nothing but will often have feathers. Angel Carrington had the largest fascinator collection on Bowen Island, perhaps in Canada and she always wore a different one when it was her turn to work at the Knick Knack Nook. Angel was ninety-three years old   Her eyesight was not good and she was unsteady on her feet but she sold more than any other cashier. This may have something to do with the cash register. She didn't like it and hardly used it. Customers placed their treasures on Angel's counter and she waved a hand over them as though making a spell. 'I will cast my eyes over these and arrive at a price' she would say. Angel's little dog stayed in a basket beside her, an exception to the No Pets Allowed rule of the Nook. Another exception was Fanny French's big yellow lab guide dog Duke. Fanny was totally blind and always came to the Nook when Angel was there.

"Hello Fanny, my dear, so good to see you. Come over to my desk and take my arm. Your glorious Duke can take us around the store and we will shop to our heart's content, said Angel carefully getting up and holding out an arm covered with bangles. "The two ladies and dog did not get very far. The door swung open and Principal Grimes came in dripping water from his black rain hat and floor length black raincoat.

"Dogs are not allowed here," he shouted.
Duke growled so quietly that no one heard but Fanny felt the vibrations on her leash. "Come in young man and stop yelling. I can assure you everything is in perfect order. Now, please stop dripping on the floor and hang your clothes up," Angel snapped.

"Where are the candles," demanded Grimes rudely.

"On that shelf, young man. But you're not shopping dripping the way you are."

"I want them all," demanded Grimes.

There were fourteen unmatched candles and small glass lanterns with candles in them. "I'll wrap them and bring the bag to you. They will be twenty dollars." This was about four times as much as a casting of eyes would normally be. Principal Grimes grabbed his bag without a thank you or goodbye and slammed the door.
"His knickers are certainly in a bunch," said Angel holding up the twenty and smiling.

CHAPTER ELEVEN: COYOTE UGLY

Josie Cameron, the twins' grandmother and her husband of fort-five years, Diefenbaker Stone lived on one of the few riding ranches on Bowen Island. Professor Stone told anyone who would listen that he kept his own last name because it was too good to for a rock doctor to lose even though he thought a man should take his bride's surname. The professor liked to cause trouble. Strider and Rohan were two of the twelve horses that lived on the ranch and only ridden when the granddaughters visited. Strider belonged to Charlie and Rohan to Eloise. This was an unusual day for the girls to visit but their grandmother wanted to talk about their principal.

"Don't tease this man," said Josie as she and the girls rode their horses along the path that ringed the big ranch.

"Oh, that ship has sailed," said Charlie laughing.

"Then you must stop. He is dangerous and not what he seems.

"Yes, Grandma," both girls said very impressed with how serious their grandmother was.

"I can't help with him."

She really was serious. Everyone on the island knew Josie Cameron had magical powers. She had more patients than both of the doctors. "Maybe Apodaca can help," said Eloise.

"I must meet your talking whale. Perhaps if I go for a swim tomorrow afternoon at Scarborough Beach."

"Can we come. We'll introduce..." the girls got no further. The horses stopped and struck the hard packed trail with front hooves. Five coyotes slunk from behind the trees and surrounded the horses and riders. Two of them dashed at Strider biting his back legs. Strider whinnied in pain, turned toward his assailants and reared up. Charlie held onto the pommel and reins but was still almost thrown. All of the coyotes came at Josie and her horse Shadowfax next. Josie whispered in her horse's ear and then Shadowfax leapt over the surprised coyotes striking two with her front hooves. They fell to the ground stunned but unhurt. The coyotes regrouped and attacked Ronan who was the smallest and youngest of the three horses. Rohan reared and bucked in terror and Eloise was thrown into a thick patch of berries. The coyotes immediately left the still terrified horse and rushed at Eloise who was their target all along. Suddenly a rusty blue bicycle crashed into the thicket of berries and a rider tumbled off. "Back away, you curs," yelled Professor Stone. The professor held a small portable vacuum.

"Oh dear, Josie said. "I'm glad to see you, of course, but I don't think these coyotes are frightened by the prospect of a spring cleaning."

"No danger of that. I have reversed the motor and thoroughly weaponized this Dustbuster," the professor said grandly. The coyotes, fully recovered from the professor's crash advanced toward Eloise who was unable to untangle herself from the berry thicket. "Say hello to my little friend, you jackals," said Professor Stone in a strange Mexican accent. He pulled a long barbecue lighter from his pocket and lit the end of the vacuum. A tiny spurt of flame appeared. The coyotes continued toward Eloise their bodies flattened to the ground, ears back and teeth bare.

"Oh, Grandpa," said Charlie, "that isn't going to work."

"It will when I set it to turbo maximum Mach eleven," said the professor turning a dial on the Dustbuster. Suddenly, a long flame shot out and singed the front paws of each coyote. Coyotes like most animals except cats and dogs were terrified of fire. As quickly as they came the coyotes were gone although it took much longer for Eloise and her grandfather to escape the berry patch.

CHAPTER TWELVE: KUROSHIO

Visitors to Bowen Island from Northern California, Oregon and Washington State are frequently outraged and jealous to see Bowenites swimming. Their weather was warmer, the sun stronger and they were nowhere near the North Pole like Bowen. The Kuroshio Current was responsible. Kuroshio means black current in Japanese, not the eating kind but a dark river of warm water that runs across the mighty Pacific Ocean. While Peter Goser mostly slept, his sailboat rode the Kuroshio through fall winter and spring. And while he slept he dreamed but the dreams were not his own. They were Tomo's dreams, Tomo, once a volcano of Yap Island but now the underwater cavern that had captured Jason and turned him into a minion, an unconscious servant. Tomo had invited Mauna Loa to his dream, the mighty Hawaiian volcano that even after so many years still spewed lava from its crater. And, of course, he had invited his friend, Mount Garibaldi or Prettyboy, as he was called.

"He will remember nothing that we say?" asked Prettyboy after introductions were made.

"He is my minion. It does not matter," said Tomo. "He came to my cavern, drank my water and now he is mine."

"You should dispose of him when he is no longer useful," said Mauna Loa.

"You may not give me advice, you are my younger," Tomo said sharply.

"You no longer have a cone, no lava and we are the same age," snapped Mauna Loa.

"We are not here to argue," said Prettyboy soothingly.

"I am here to make you a new volcano, Prettyboy. I am not sure why Tomo is here. He is nothing but a cave."

"He is my friend and he is here to advise me. He tells me I should listen to you."

"Tomo is wise. It is good that he is here. I will give you the lava that you require; I have more than I need."

"That is unfair while I have none," complained Tomo who had lost his cone millions of years ago.

"Your lava may return someday, my friend," said Mauna Loa, "you are too far away for me to help. First Prettyboy, you must rid your Bowen Island of its humans."

"Surely, that is not necessary. It will take too long and please call me Garibaldi."

"Time is nothing to a volcano," cautioned Tomo, "you must listen to your benefactor."

"Not long ago," said Mauna Loa, "I sent lava out of my cone to improve its beauty. The foolish humans nearby feared their town would burn and sent airplanes to drop bombs on me. It is a lesson I will never forget. Their bombs are much more powerful now. My friend Fuji says one bomb can destroy an entire volcano. No, young Prettyboy, the humans will not care if a new volcano forms on an empty island. I will give you all the lava you wish for when the last human leaves Bowen Island."

"My plan must work then," said Prettyboy, "I will speed it up. Your minion, Tomo will help."

"He is your minion now, my friend," said Tomo. "What will you call your new volcano?"

"It will certainly not be Prettyboy," said Prettyboy. "My old name of Garibaldi I have never liked. My new volcano will be called Thunderdome."

CHAPTER THIRTEEN: ROAD TRIP

If killer whales had or needed police their detectives would use the orcas' dorsal fin for identification. Just like the human hand all dorsal fins are different although it has no fingers or opposable thumb. The finger bones of a killer whale are in the front fins and don't do much at all. If they did perhaps it would be the killer whales that were flying around the earth and spending half their time on computers. The dorsal fin was also handy for a human rider to hold onto. This didn't happen very often but it was happening today. Josie Cameron and Apodaca had been swimming and talking for almost an hour while the girls and their grandfather listened politely. The two grandmothers were now old friends and the desirability of Diefenbaker Stone's presence had been remarked on twice. They were waiting for three of Apodaca's granddaughters to show up. Apodaca had sent a message to a passing pod that would pass it along to her pod. "Killer whales really are quite conscientious about such things as delivering messages," Apodaca assured Josie who was holding onto her dorsal and enjoying the warm sun on Apodaca's back.

"Tell me about these bears again," said Josie.

"Just four bears, as I said," said Apodaca, "big and stupid and mean, I'm sure."

"I'm really more interested in who brought them."

"A young man in a sailboat. He didn't seem at all scared of the bears. They just jumped off the boat when he got close to the island and swam to shore. He turned his boat around and headed up the Sound toward Squamish."

"Then that's where we'll go. Oh, look. These splendid whales must be your granddaughters."

"More like two granddaughters and one disobedient grandson," said Apodaca swimming over to her grandchildren and butting them each gently on their mouths. "Josie, this is Cecelia and Peg and this big fellow is Bruno who I have never missed because he simply won't go away like all my other grandsons."

"Can I ride Bruno please," said Charlie who had swum over along with Eloise and their grandfather.

"Don't tell me that's why we're here, Grams," said Bruno.

"And if it is," said Apodaca with a little menace in her voice.

"Then I say hop on little girl," said Bruno submerging so Charlie could swim onto his back.

"I'm not a little girl," said Charlie grabbing Bruno's dorsal fin.

"I have sisters. I should have known better."

"Call me Ishmael," said the professor to Peg as he slid onto her back. "Not my name of course which is Diefenbaker but the start of a tale about a man and a whale and my favorite story in the world. I will tell it to you as we journey."

"Grandma," warned Eloise who was now on Cecilia's back and had heard her grandfather's favorite story many times, "don't let grandpa tell that story, Ishmael's leg gets bitten off by a you know what."

"Dear, tell the young whales about the geology of the Sound. That would be much more appropriate," said Josie with a little menace in her voice too.

"Quite right, my dear. The small island you see in front of you, Boyer Island is amazingly a rock drumlin, one of the few such of its kind in the world. Formed by glaciers and shaped like a teardrop it tells us many things."

"Where are we going Grandma," said Charlie while her grandfather droned on unaware of the interruption and that his audience had abandoned him.

"Why, to find that sailboat which I suspect is anchored near Squamish."

"You heard my friend," said Apodaca.

The whales and riders sped away as fast as a motorboat; as they passed Finnisterre Island just before they would turn up the Sound and away from Bowen, two dolphins raced past them. Behind the terrified dolphins were two jet-skis in pursuit, like motorcycles on water skipping across the waves. Two young men, beers in hand, were chasing the dolphins and yelling, 'not so fast now, are you Flipper'.

"Get them girls," yelled Apodaca.

Cecelia, Peg and Bruno jumped out of the water and began the chase. The dolphins were fast and the jet skis faster but the killer whales were faster still. The twins and their grandfather held on for dear life as they quickly closed the gap with the jet skis. Bruno and Charlie reached the motorboats first and Bruno launched himself totally out of the water. When he came down a huge wave washed over the nearest jet-ski rolling it onto its side. Peg and Cecelia did the same to the remaining jet-ski. The young men were floating in water safe in their life jackets. The beers were nowhere in sight.

"They look tasty," said Bruno clicking his big teeth.

"Oh, you can't eat them," said Apodaca who caught up.

"Perhaps just their legs," suggested Josie.

"If they promise not to chase dolphins," said Bruno still clicking his teeth, "I'll let them go."

CHAPTER FOURTEEN: WIND RIDERS

Land usually shrinks. It happens slowly and is hard to notice. Sometimes the oceans rise or heavy rains wash the land away. Squamish was different. Every year the town grew into the Sound. A lot. People noticed; sometimes three feet sometimes six. It rained buckets in Squamish and the Squamish River dumped fallen trees, rocks and dirt into the Sound. Much of it came from the collapsed cone of Mount Garibaldi. The Native People called Garibaldi the Grimy One because so much debris washed down its slopes. Most of this happened during the rainy months in the fall and winter. It was late spring now and Squamish Harbour, the very tip of Howe Sound was filled with all manner of small boats. Most of them belonged to wind-sport athletes all waiting for the Squamish wind to blow. There were windsurfers, parasailing rigs and kite surfers lounging impatiently on their boats looking about for signs of wind.

"Young Bruno, if you're through eating salmon," said Professor Stone, "I had no idea a killer whale ate so much, I will tell you about the glorious esker." Bruno's huge eyelids became heavy and closed over his black eyes. "An esker can be hundreds of miles long. I have measured many, although any esker around here would be on the ocean floor. Bruno, wake up Bruno, you must be my underwater eyes and find the local esker for me."

"Diefenbaker, stop pestering poor Bruno," said his wife. "Apodaca says that is the sailboat we're looking for."

"I see no one on board."

"I will swim over to the dock and untie the ropes. I suggest you and the twins join me on Apodaca's back. Your rides will soon be underwater."

Bruno, Peg and Cecelia disappeared and soon the sailboat floated out into the clear water of the Sound as though a motor were pushing it. Apodaca swam to the boat's side and Josie, Diefenbaker and the twins scrambled over its railing.

"There is somebody on board," said Eloise.

"It must be the young man who brought the bears," said Josie as she walked over to Jason Goser who was asleep or unconscious on the deck. Josie knelt and felt his forehead. He's in a trance. Oh, no," she whispered, suddenly standing and clutching her hands to her chest. "This young man is someone's minion. Someone very powerful."

Before another word could be said a cold bucket of seawater splashed on Jason's face. "Always works," said the professor.

"You know not what you do, Diefenbaker Stone," said Josie who only used her husband's full name when she was irritated. Jason coughed, sputtered and opened his eyes. The professor wisely said nothing. Josie knelt again and put both hands on Jason's forehead. "His last memory that is his own is exploring a cave."

"He's a spelunker," said Diefenbaker clapping his hands. "I once was a marvelous spelunker. I know just what he needs." The professor dove into the water and swam toward town.

"I want two parasailing rigs each with a two man harness," said Professor Stone to the startled crowd in the

Squamish Water Sports store. The professor walked over to a large blackboard that said 'Today's Conditions, erased everything on the board and began scribbling furiously.

"Hey man," the store's owner said. "You can't do that. Those are the 'Wind Guru's' words. He knows the wind."

"Today," said the professor still writing in a cloud of chalk dust, "the Wind Guru is wrong. The Squamish will begin blowing at six o'clock and last until morning. The Willawaw is as predictable as the tides."

The Squamish Wind did start to blow at six. Three great gusts fell off the frigid top of Mount Garibaldi and tore through the town before screaming down Howe Sound. Professor Stone unrolled the two big balloon-like sails on the deck of the sailboat under the watchful eye of his wife. Josie shook her head. "You have a lot of dangerous ideas, Diefenbaker Stone," said his wife, "and even more stupid ones. This appears to be both stupid and dangerous."

"I can assure you, sweetheart," said the professor who liked to use 'sweetheart' when Josie called him by his full name, "parasailing is as safe as walking when done slowly and carefully. Young Jason, the twins and I will get in the parasailing harnesses and Bruno will tow us."

"So this is what you think Jason needs," Diefenbaker Stone, "I assume because he is a spelunker and you know spelunkers."

"Precisely, sweetheart. A spelunker craves adventure. This will bring the real Jason back."

"It actually makes some sense. But there's no way under the sun that you are taking my granddaughters up in that contraption."

"And there's no way that Bruno is towing," said Apodaca.

"But Bruno can swim as fast as a galloping horse," protested the professor.

"I'm still pretty fast myself, said Apodaca. "If there is towing to be done, I will do it."

Charlie and Eloise strapped themselves into the parasailing harness as quickly as possible both not believing that their grandmother was going to allow this amazing adventure and that she was going as well. Professor Stone dragged a still stunned Jason over and secured him next to Eloise while Josie strapped herself next to Charlie.

"This is going to be amazing, Grandma," said Charlie.

"Amazing and a bit dangerous," said Josie, "but I think we have to take some chances."

"Start off at about half speed, Apodaca," said the professor. "That should be fast enough to lift the sails into the air and pull our four wind riders behind it."

Apodaca set off swimming strongly. First the two giant parachute-like sails rose from the sailboat's deck and climbed quickly into the air; then the two harnesses one with Josie and Charlie and the other with Eloise and Jason climbed into the air. "We're flying," screamed Eloise." The weight of the sails and gliders slowly Apodaca down considerably and she swished her great tail even harder. The sails lifted more into the air and the girls discovered they could move from side to side using their arms as rudders.

"Can we go all the way to Bowen Island, Grandma," asked Charlie.

"Right to Scarborough Beach," said Josie not bothering to hide her excitement. "Oh, isn't this grand." When it became clear that they weren't coming back, Bruno and Professor Stone gave chase while Peg and Cecelia headed back to their pod.

"Hey Ishmael," said Bruno when they had caught up, "why don't you tell me that story."

CHAPTER FIFTEEN: ONE TOO MANY FARTS

Most guide dogs for the blind were Labrador Retrievers. Labs were smart, calm and knew as many words as most people. Fanny talked to her dog Duke but Duke never talked back. Until now, now he wouldn't shut up.

"We have a visitor today, class," said Principal Grimes. "She is here to demonstrate an exception to the Survival of the Fittest scientific law that I have taught you. Our visitor today is blind which makes her anything but one of the fittest. In the old days the blind if they lived at all lived horrible short lives. We are all fortunate to live in a world of abundance where we can look after and provide for those who are unable to do so for themselves.

"Why are there chickens if survival of the fittest is a scientific law," said Charlie without raising her hand. "Chickens can't fly, can't fight, are stupid and almost every animal likes to eat them. How did they ever survive from old times."

"Please say good morning to our guest," said Principal Grimes ignoring Charlie, "Fanny Harper and her guide dog, Duke."

Duke entered first, stopped, looked at Principal Grimes and farted long and loudly. For a while the classroom didn't smell like the principal. The entire class laughed in spite of their principal's glare and Eloise whispered, "I love that dog."

"Dogs of course belong outside. They are unclean and poorly behaved. We make an exception for our guest," said Principal Grimes unhappily.

Duke led Fanny to the head of the classroom. "Hello class," she said. "Thank you for inviting me and Duke. I would like to correct something your principal said if I may Principal Grimes."

"Of course," said the principal looking cruelly at the unknowing Fanny,

"In old days blind people were often cared for quite well because people thought them wise and able to see the future. I don't know if that's survival of the fittest but blind people often lived quite well.

The mood of Principal Grimes did not improve during Fanny's talk to the Grade Seven class. Duke slept nosily at her feet and farted twice more. The principal was much happier when the class was dismissed and his students walked out chattering. Eloise and Charlie formed part of a large group that accompanied Fanny and Duke as they left the school. "Could we walk home with you, Fanny; our kayak is in Deep Bay which is right by the Home for the Blind,' said Charlie.

"That would be perfect. Your principal didn't seem that happy with my talk."

"He doesn't like anybody. Can Duke talk," asked Eloise.

"So, you know about that," answered Duke.

"All the animals on Bowen talk now," said Charlie.

"Well, I'm relieved it isn't just me," said Duke. "I was beginning to think one of us was nuts. Your principal smells worse than my farts."

"He says it's a medical condition," said Eloise. "But I think it's because he's basically a volcano."

"How can he be a volcano," said Fanny

"It's all kinds of weird magic and stuff," said Charlie, "talking animals and volcanoes, it's all connected. He even wants to turn Bowen Island into a volcano."

"Well, we can't let that...." Fanny got no further. As they walked down the empty street the same four coyotes dashed out and attacked. The smaller coyotes knocked Duke on his side and two of them grabbed by him the throat. Charlie and Eloise hit the coyotes with their backpacks and Fanny yelled for help. It was over quickly and Duke lay still, blood oozing from the punctures in his neck. The coyotes ran away into the forest as though their job was done.

"Oh, Fanny," sobbed Eloise, "I think he's dead."

"Grandma, come quickly," said Charlie into her cell phone. "We're by the Home for the Blind."

In minutes Josie screeched to a stop in her old Jeep 4X4. Nothing was far away on Bowen. She held Duke's lifeless head between her hands and turned to look at the West Lion Mountain, its late spring snow shining bright golden yellow in the setting sun. Josie's lips moved but she made no sign. Duke's tail wagged and he opened his eyes.

"You're awesome Grandma," said Eloise.

"You can thank the West and the East Lion Mountains. The Lions watch over all of Howe Sound. You two should know this."

"Well, I thank you and the Lions," said Duke springing up. "And I blame that smelly principal. I just know he was behind this. Probably payback for farting on him."

"He was certainly behind this," said Josie. The coyotes are his minions as are all the unwanted animals coming over to the island. I have told you and I tell you all again; he is dangerous, do not trifle with him and most certainly do not fart on him."

"We promise," said Eloise and Charlie.

CHAPTER SIXTEEN: PINEAPPLE EXPRESS

Weather to most people is boring. This is why weather experts or meteorologists make special names for storms like Polar Vortex and Cyclone Bomb or Pineapple Express to make weather more exciting. The Pineapple Express is a big storm that starts in Hawaii and travels quickly to the west coast of North America. There are no pineapples involved. It has been described as a river in the sky. That is how much water is in its thick dark clouds.

Pineapple Expresses usually happens in the fall and winter but this particular one was sweeping across the mighty Pacific Ocean in spring. It was the biggest ever and Mauna Loa wanted it as a girt for Prettboy and what Mauna wants Mauna gets. The massive clouds sucked up the warm Pacific Ocean water of Hawaii and scurried across waves until reaching the mountains of Howe Sound. It was here that the great river of water poured on the mountain peaks, in particular Mount Garibaldi, especially Mount Garibaldi. Snow melted and on Mount Garibaldi its ancient glacier of ice turned to water. Lose lava rocks and dirt washed down into the valleys and choked the Squamish River. The force of the swollen river pushed the rocks and dirt into the narrow neck of Howe Sound. The land grew. The storm went on for two weeks never weakening. The land grew and grew until it stretched from island to island all the way to Bowen. It was hidden and underwater at high tide but at low tide it was a land bridge that could be walked from the town of Squamish to Hood Point, the northern most point on Bowen Island. Wolves, bears, mountain lions, coyotes came by the hundreds on the new land bridge all to eat the peaceful creatures of Bowen Island.

The Pineapple Express flooding was duck soup to Killarney Kit. Beavers loved water--the more the better. Water meant bigger, higher dams and a deeper wider canal around the beaver lodge. Canals made great escape routes in case of danger or a way to find some peace away from the lodge. Lately, ever since the animals began to talk, the lodge was a noisy place and Killarney Kit didn't care for speech. Waste of time. Now, his wife talked all the time—waste of time. The kits wouldn't stop talking—big waste of time. All that the animals of Killarney Lake wanted to do now was talk. Who got eaten, what trees the mountain lions were sleeping in and how many eggs the raccoons had stolen. Of course Kit and family were safe in their lodge with its underwater entrance; as long as no otters made the short walk from the ocean to Killarney Lake. Otters could swim underwater and knew all about beaver lodges and the underwater entrance. They loved to eat young kits. Of course, mountain lions and coyotes found otters rather tasty which probably made the short walk from the ocean somewhat dangerous. Kit doubted that otters would bother him even if they could swim safely all the way to his lodge entrance on account of the new lodge that had risen up three days ago slightly bigger and altogether far to close to Kit's beautiful lodge. It was scary. Hot smelly mud bubbled up every day just before noon and when it dried the new lodge got bigger and closer. Killarney Kit wondered in horror if he was going to have to move. He chewed down a tree that fell between the two lodges and felt much better.

CHAPTER SEVENTEEN: DOG DAYS

Charlie, Eloise and Duke walked down the main street of Snug Cove. Eloise wore a scary metal hook on her right hand and a huge black hat with a feathery plume. The hat and hook didn't look out of place with her puffy frilly white shirt, black tights and knee length black boots. Nor did the bushy mustache and big fake nose. Charlie wore tights as well but a hunter green that matched her shirt. Over the shirt she wore a brown vest that matched her small felt hat. It also had a feather but not as big as her sister's. On her feet were beige suede Peter Pan Getaway boots. Duke walked uncomfortably with a teal green tutu around his hindquarters. Two white wings bobbed across his back and a blond wig that he was unable to shake off was strapped to his head. Nobody in town gave them a second look. Of course, the people and dogs that they passed were dressed as the Three Musketeer, Batman and Robin, the Three Little Pigs and Harry Potter and friends. It was Bowen Island's Dog Days of Summer parade and contest and Peter Pan, Captain Hook and Tinkerbell planned to win best costume. The parade started almost half an hour late, as do most things on Bowen. It started in the BICS parking lot and ended up at the ferry terminal and was over in record time. There just weren't many people and dogs in the parade or people left to watch. Bowen was losing it population, a bunch every day. As the parade moved into the Crippen Park Fairgrounds moving trucks and cars filled with belongs took their place in line for the next ferry off the island. Some the families were missing their beloved pets and they all had frightening stories about bears, coyotes, mountain lions and raccoons.

Dog Days of Summer best costume was decided at the big Crippen Park gazebo in the center of the fairground. All the participants stood in the gazebo while the parade marshal held her hand over each costumed duo and trio. The crowd clapped, yelled and whistled for their favorite. There were no rules to this just noise and lots of it. The Neverland bunch won easily and both Charlie and Eloise smiled modestly thinking it was their clever costume that, by itself, had earned the blue ribbon. Duke said nothing like the good sport that he was, but he knew who was the star of their act.

Every proper parade had a fire truck and on Bowen it was the Bowen Island Volunteer Fire Department. After the award ceremonies the volunteers set up a large barbecue and prepared hamburgers, hotdogs and tofu lookalikes. Tinkerbell, Batman and Harry Potter crowded around hoping for handouts or droppings from careless eaters. It was a happy but small crowd and nobody noticed the six bears walk out of the forest that bordered the park. Duke smelled them over the aroma of the barbecues. Bears really stink. At the edge of the forest stood Principal Grimes waving his hands at the bears as though he was conducing an orchestra. Josie, the oldest fireman or firewomen for that matter was busy flipping burgers and was the fist to notice the bears. "Looks like we've got a fire, guys," she said pointing at the advancing bears. Josie was the unofficial fire chief and always gave the orders. "Connect a hose to the main hydrant. Make that two hoses." The fire crew jumped to action and both hoses were connected and spewing long jets of water in a minute. "Let those nasty bears have it," said Josie. Bears don't mind water and even the strong stream from the hoses couldn't knock them down. But bears had sensitive noses and when Josie told her crew so aim at their snouts the battle of Crippen Park was over in a hurry. "Chase them down guys," said Josie, "and give Principal Grimes a bath while you're at it." The chase never happened. The ground began to rapidly but gently shake. Principal Grimes screamed, "No!" and ran to the parking lot.

"To the Jeep, Diefenbaker," Josie yelled to her husband who was eating his second hotdog in spite of the excitement. "Let's follow this smelly evildoer and find out what he's up to."

"We're coming too," said Eloise and Charlie.

"I can stay here," Duke said who had his own hotdog.

CHAPTER EIGHTEEN: SHAKE AND BAKE

Hood Point is the northern tip of Bowen Island. On a clear day the entire narrowing Sound can be seen, a kind of funnel that ends at its tip in the town of Squamish; behind Squamish the volcano Garibaldi towers and the wilds of British Columbia. Quiet, almost uninhabited Hood Point was now the busy entrance point for the many fierce and hungry animals that travelled the newly formed land bridge. Most people would have been terrified by the steady stream of bears, mountain lions, wolves and coyotes although Principal Grimes would have smiled at the predators if he knew how to smile; after all he was their master. Besides, Grimes was too busy to smile. He was on his knees hurriedly arranging the assortment of candles that he had bought from the Nook. When they were in a large circle around him he lit them all and began to chant:
Lava, lava, boil and rise
Form a cone that reaches the skies

Two more verses remained to be said to invoke the volcanic eruption that the principal so craved but it was not to be as Josie's Jeep screeched to a halt in front of him. Rocks sprayed across his circle knocking over three of the candles.

"You will pay dearly for this, witch," snarled Grimes.

Josie and the twins jumped out of the Jeep followed by Diefenbaker who was somewhat tangled in his seatbelt.

"It's time for you to leave this island, Prettyboy," said Josie.

"You may not command me, human. It is you who must leave or burn from the fire of my lava."

"Take his candles, girls." The twins ran toward the circle but before they could take two steps four hissing mountain lions jumped in front.

"My cats are hungry," said Grimes evilly.

The ground that was still gently shaking began to toss and jump. The cougars that had been just about to jump sank to their bellies. Eloise and Charlie waved their outstretched arms as though they were on a tightrope and their grandfather fell to the ground in a heap, "Most unusual," he muttered, "a sustained earthquake that fluctuates in intensity. Josie stood still and totally unmoved.

Suddenly, two old men appeared within the circles. Each was dressed in flowing white robes and their white beards nearly reached the ground. Their long white hair was tied in many cornrows each with a sparkling diamond or ruby at its end. "You must go, Prettyboy," they said in unison to Principal Grimes.

"Why are you here, Comova and Comata. You do not belong here. You have your own volcanoes and areas. Howe Sound is mine."

"You do not need to worry about us, Prettyboy," said Comata. "It appears you are fighting Captain Hook and Peter Pan. Peter Pan never loses."

"You talk nonsense, old man. These are just schoolgirls and it is you who must go."

"We have called a meeting of the Ring of Fire," said Comova. "Mauna Loa's lava will not flow and you must leave this island now."

"Mauna Loa is too powerful to stop.",

"You are a fool," shouted Comata in a deep booming voice. "I am more powerful, bigger and older than Mauna

Loa. She will not challenge me. You should not challenge me."

"He must be Mount Rainier," Diefenbaker muttered to himself.

"This is not your area, old man," said Prettyboy.

"Everything is my area. Farther then the eye can see would feel the wrath of my eruption. Your pathetic half cone volcano would be buried in my ash. Leave. Leave now," thundered Comata.

"No, I refuse. You have no power."

"Look to your volcano, Prettyboy," said Comata, " It is filling with my lava. This is not Mauna Loa's lava as you had hoped. It is mine and soon your volcano will be mine."

"Stop, I will leave," whimpered Prettyboy. Principal Grimes groaned loudly as his clothes, beard and hair began to smoke. Flame flickered out of his mouth and nose.

"Take your animals with you," said Comova. "They have an hour to cross the land bridge before it is destroyed."

"Poor Principal Grimes," said Charlie.

"Do not shed a tear, Peter Pan," said Comata. "Fire cannot hurt him.'

CHAPTER NINETEEN: BEAR BUTT SMACKDOWN

"Who were those guys," asked Eloise after the two old men had left.

"And why was their hair in cornrows and why did one of them think we were Peter Pan and Captain Hook," added Charlie.

"No idea about the cornrows, girls," answered Josie. "I'm pretty sure the older one was a Disney fan."

"Let me take it from here," said Diefenbaker.

"You do that, dear. Girls, I think we should all sit down."

"Clearly," began Diefenbaker, "Comova is Mount Baker or at least the old man was Mount Baker's avatar. Comata is Mount Rainier. As I'm sure you know Baker and Rainier are the two largest volcanoes in Washington State. Rainier, of course is one of the biggest in the United States. You are dressed like Peter Pan and Captain Hook girls, what was Comata supposed to think."

"Charlie, Eloise," a distant yell came from the ocean. Josie and the girls ran to the jagged rocks of Hood Point overlooking the beach.

"But I'm not finished," sputtered Diefenbaker.

"Apodaca," said Eloise, "what are you doing here?"

"Comova, who was grumpy even for him, ordered me to come. He said all the nasty animals are leaving Bowen Island and that I must supervise. Oh, he also said that the land bridge is about to fall to the ocean bottom. Why are you dressed like a pirate and a little boy?"

"Do you need our help," said Eloise waving her hook.

"I've got help, Bruno is coming. He says he wants to eat a bear although as far as I know he just eats salmon."

"Here they come," said Charlie pointing at the animals that were just running onto the land bridge. The rising tide was lapping over the huge pile of rocks and the animals' feet splashed the ocean water as they ran. Four bears led the way, trotting slowly on all four paws and growling angrily at each other. Mountain lions, coyotes, raccoons and wolves crowded behind them unable to pass the bulky bears who took up the entire width of the land bridge. Suddenly, Bruno's huge body flew out of the water and soared over the land bridge. Bruno slapped the biggest bear's butt with his tail as he passed. The bear howled in pain, surprise and fear. Bears were used to being the biggest animal in the forest. A black and white flying whale four times their size with enormous white teeth was an unpleasant surprise. The bears ran but not fast enough for Bruno. He turned around and leapt over the land bridge again, this time slapping a different bear's butt.

The earth's shaking grew more rapid and rocks started to slide off the land bridge into the ocean. The water, unable to form waves, popped like popcorn.

"Comova said this would happen," shouted Apodaca. "He said he'd stop it once all the animals are across and the land bridge is gone."

"He'd better stop it soon," said Eloise, "I'm getting sick to my stomach."

"I think Bruno can stop smacking the bears," said Charlie. "They're going as fast as they can."

"Oh, Bruno is going to keep doing that until all the animals are across," said Apodaca. "He's having fun."

Bruno, the bears and all the other nasty animals soon disappeared from sight as they followed the land bridge into the narrowing Sound.

"Is our island going to be safe now so all the people can move back," said Charlie.

"Prettyboy Grimes is gone for good, I think," said Josie, "and the animals will have no way to get back. I think Bowen Island is absolutely safe."

"Nothing is safe in the Ring of Fire," said Diefenbaker solemnly.

"Is that really what you want to say, dear," said Josie with a hint of a very nasty look.

"Don't worry, girls," said their grandfather smiling at his wife. "I'm sure nothing can possibly go wrong as long as we have two volcanoes looking after us."

"I'm going to say goodbye," said Apodaca. "When the bridge is gone we won't be able to speak to each other anymore."

"You mean we won't see you again," said Eloise sadly.

"Maybe there will be another emergency," said Charlie hopefully.

"I'll still scratch my belly at Scarborough Beach and you never know about emergencies. After all, like your grandfather says: There's always something happening in the Ring of Fire."

ABOUT THE AUTHOR

Rodger Beals was an amazing father, husband and friend. Rodger knew how to turn a phrase and his dog Duke always knew how to time a fart. Rodger's wit is missed by many, but he left us this book to spread some of his amazing imagination and humour through the world.

Made in the USA
San Bernardino, CA
24 December 2018